Burnish Me Bright

Burnish Me Bright

by Julia Cunningham
Pictures by Don Freeman
Pantheon Books

WITH SILENT LOVE FOR
*Lydia and Don Freeman
and Emily Lawrence Newton*
THE MAGICIANS

Burnish me bright before the night comes tarnishing

THE BOOK OF PERSONS

Burnish Me Bright

❧ *One* ❧

The old man had just sat down on his work stool to rest from his morning set of exercises and was looking with some sadness at his crooked fingers. These were the hands, this the body, that had mirrored all the moods and magic of living. On stage they had given him the grace and the power to be everything, everybody: birds, animals, clowns, death, childhood, sweepers, kings, joy— all and any. The power to tell it without words, with only movement, had waited behind the quiet of these long arms and legs, this instrument that was now inhabited by the lameness of old age.

He smiled and spoke to himself. "Monsieur Hilaire, a few yesterdays ago you were the greatest mime in the world. Wasn't that enough?"

A thin sound of clapping, two hands hitting sharply together this winter morning, came from somewhere outside his sadness, his house, and greeted his sitting down. He regretted for this one piercing moment the thousands of hands in hundreds of theaters that would no longer bring him back to bow once more before the curtain.

He got up and looked for his last audience. There behind the glass door that led to the little terrace he saw a boy. His shoulders were hunched high under his ragged jacket, his boney face, shaped like a spade, was bright past its pallor with smiling, and his hands, now still, were clasped tight together in delight.

Monsieur Hilaire went to the door and opened it wide. "Come in! Come in!"

The boy seemed startled.

"Quickly, child, quickly! I'm inviting you, not the wind." And when the boy simply stood, Monsieur Hilaire reached one arm outside, gripped him by the sleeve, and pulled him into the room. "You're not afraid of me. You couldn't be." He propelled the boy to the high fire. "Warm yourself, *mon petit*. What brought you out? Some sort of adventure?"

The old man indicated a little stool to one side of the hearth and then seated himself in the armchair nearest the flames. He noted the smallness, the shabbiness of the boy's coat, the droop of his shorts that were man-sized trousers cut off, the sandals mended with bits of string. "I'm puzzled," he said. "I don't know you but I've seen you somewhere before."

The boy sidled two steps away. His right leg knocked against the stool but he did not take his eyes from the man's face.

Monsieur Hilaire suddenly slapped his hand on his knee. "I know! Of course! You live with Madame Fer at the old Reglaude place!" He stopped talking for a moment, and instead looked so intently that the boy turned

4

his head as if to hide from this new speech. "But you are mute. Now I remember. And here I sit bothering you with questions you can't answer."

Something—the candor or the kindness—made the boy slowly move forward and lower himself onto the stool. His gaze now returned to the old man's.

"That's better. Now we can continue our conversation. But perhaps you are hungry? I was just about to have a bowl of soup. Shall we share it?"

The boy shook his head.

"Next time, then. And maybe it could be chicken with salad and a glass of good wine." Monsieur Hilaire resettled himself in his chair. "I get lonely here sometimes. It's good to have company. I wish I knew your name. It strengthens a friendship to exchange names. Mine is Hercule Hilaire. A rather foolish combination, don't you agree? But when I became well enough known to drop the first name, I did. The playbills and posters took on more distinction with the single word."

The boy was now studying the light cover of ash dust that coated the hearth. Then, warily, with rapid side glances at the old man, he began, with his forefinger, to write in it in large letters.

"So they let you go to school, did they? I'm glad. Our villagers are none too cordial to whomever is different than themselves. And I perceive that you are different. Nothing to do with not being able to speak, you understand. It's a kind of feeling I have."

The boy sat up again. Monsieur Hilaire read what he had written. "Auguste. So that's who you are!" He laughed, ignoring the boy's anxiety. "I once knew a clown named Auguste. One of the finest. He taught me a great deal. Oh, I never met him, just watched. I used to save whatever money I could scrape up doing errands and the like and spend it all on cheap seats at his circus." He came back from the memory. "So your name is already honored." He gently put his hand forward. "Now that we are known to each other, let's shake hands."

With the swiftness of a flying shadow a smile passed over the boy's face and before it vanished he stretched out his arm and their two hands met.

"That's better. Now for that soup." Monsieur Hilaire rose and went to the shallow alcove at the far end of the room. "Why don't you look around while the soup decides to bubble? You may find a few things of interest to you. And don't neglect the second story. This is a very old house and I suspect was once the lodge of a château. Go on—explore."

He disappeared into the alcove.

For ten minutes, only the soft hissing of the gas under the soup kettle competed with the rushing of the wind in the shutters. The boy, wherever he was, made no sound. No floor board cracked. No stair squeaked.

The near silence broke with a pounding at the front door. Monsieur Hilaire lowered the gas and then opened the door to what at first looked like a shawled and sweatered stump. But the form had a voice, graveled and loud. "Where is he? Where did that wretch get to?"

"Won't you come in, Madame Fer?"

The woman entered and stared up at the grave severity of the old man's face. She thrust out her hand.

"Sorry, sir, to barge in like this but that boy is nothing but misery. He runs off."

"Where is who, madame?" asked Monsieur Hilaire, ignoring her outburst. "Do sit down, please. Would you take a glass of wine?"

Her lumpy face reddened. "No thank you, monsieur," was all she could get past her embarrassment. She sat on the edge of the nearest chair, then continued. "The mute boy. He was seen coming this way."

"Tell me about this boy, madame," asked Monsieur Hilaire, purposely avoiding an answer. "His name is Auguste, is it not?"

"Someone labeled him, yes. Was found under a bush, that one. Somebody's bastard—no one knows whose, though there was a lot of talk at the time. We handed him around for a few years until he was big enough to work and then I took him in. Dumb he is, dumb as a stone. Not normal. Never cried or laughed or so much as grunted." She was losing her awareness of the tall aristocrat beside her, though she had never conversed with him before. He kept clear of the village and only appeared on market days to buy food for the week. Her anger began to build again. "He owes me. I give him enough to eat, a bed-down in the stable, and I even let him go to school when the farm work let up in the winter, only he quit after the fourth year."

"Why?" asked Monsieur Hilaire.

"Never asked," she replied defensively. "Heard there was trouble between him and the other children. Fights or something."

The old man's hands flexed as he visualized the possible horrors of the play yard.

"As I said before—he owes me, plenty. And he's never even tried to thank me, not once, not with a smile or a gesture. An animal shows more gratitude. Now he's taken to never even looking at me."

"Are you cruel to him, Madame Fer?" The question was gentle.

"Cruel—what's cruel? He got the same number of beatings any bad child gets. That's the way life is for us. No fancy manners. No time for them." She pointed to the portrait over the fireplace. "Our houses don't have pictures in them, monsieur. Can't eat canvas."

"But from what I hear you have a very prosperous farm."

"I put away my money, monsieur. When it's spent it's gone." She got up. "And time is waste, too. Where is he?"

"I don't know," said the old man. He went to the door. "Good day, madame." His tone of command walked her out, but her last sentence lingered in the room—"If he comes here you tell him the next time he runs away I'll tie him to a cow stall!"

After she had gone out of sight the old man called up the stair well, "Auguste? You can come down now!"

There was no reply. Monsieur Hilaire shrugged at his foolishness. Of course, the boy couldn't answer if he wanted to. Slowly, the backs of his legs aching a little, he ascended the stairs.

The two small whitewashed bedrooms were vacant. The old man sighed at the foot of the steep flight that led to the attic. "Auguste!" he tried again. "The soup is ready! Show yourself, boy, and save my old bones a journey."

But the dark entrance to the loft remained empty.

Monsieur Hilaire smiled to himself. Perhaps if he made a role out of being more ancient than he was the ordeal would be easier. He gave himself a moment to shrink. He curved the fingers of his left hand around the head of an imaginary walking stick. He dropped his head into a slight palsy. A hump seemed to form on his back. Carefully he slid his right foot up and onto the first board. Had anyone been watching they might have believed him incapable of achieving the second. But he did, so painfully, so truly, he knew he would remember this anonymous performance with pleasure.

At last he reached the doorway. He released his body once more into tallness. He stood silent, scanning the familiar outlines of the two costume trunks, the broken harp that had been his mother's, the bookshelf filled

with yellowed theater programs. And then he saw the boy. He was flattened fast against a windowless wall, his arms spread-eagled as though to merge with the beams behind him. His face gleamed white with fright.

Monsieur Hilaire stayed where he was. "She is gone, Auguste. I sent her away. You can relax now."

There was no change in the boy's rigidity.

The old man stepped just inside the threshold. He stretched out his own arms in imitation of the boy's and pressed back against the air behind him, making it seem also like a wall. His chest became concave, even his face seemed to revert to youngness, to pinch into fear.

Suddenly the boy's arms fell to his sides and he impulsively ran to the old man, as though to comfort him. He stopped short one foot away.

Monsieur Hilaire gently resumed himself. "You see how fear looks?" he said. "Come now, help me down to the living room or my slowness will burn the soup."

A few minutes later the two of them sat across from each other at the oak table, spooning up the savory liquid. When they had finished, the boy's eyes began to take in what surrounded him. Past the paintings and the prints, past the few pieces of worn furniture, past the wall of books, his gaze halted at the ceiling-high mirror.

"Would you like to see my partner?" asked the old man.

The boy frowned.

"Come." Monsieur Hilaire waited until Auguste cautiously followed him to the oblong of glass. "Stand a little to one side, if you please." The man bowed like a courtier, low, with a sweep of his right arm. "May I present Auguste? Auguste, Hilaire." The reflection met the bow.

"Step forward," said the mime. The boy obeyed. For an instant he stared at his image. Then he too lowered his body into an answering reverence.

"Now we are four, our partners and ourselves, and by the look of it, very well met." He turned from the mirror. "You have the gift of grace, Auguste," he said solemnly. "Have you also the vision?" He laughed. "But I am indeed a fool. Talk never told it." He faced the mirror again. "Shall I ask my partner to show you a bird?"

Auguste nodded shyly.

"A bird of prey—a hawk? An ostrich? A humming-bird? A crow?"

But, as though a cloak had fallen from his shoulders, he seemed to have removed himself from the presence of the boy, the structure of the room, the boundary of the house. His arms became wings, his feet claws. He was a hawk circling in a dark sky. Then, as he wheeled downward he became smaller, became the victim. He fluttered. He weakened. He alighted on an invisible branch and panted for strength. But the shadow of the hawk still seemed to overcast him. His mouth opened in soundless terror. It was a beak.

The boy, frozen in this enchantment, suddenly rushed at the helplessness of the grounded bird, and spreading himself as wide as he could, became a shield, his back vulnerable to the hawk.

The moment held, then broke.

Monsieur Hilaire let out a long breath. "You believed it and you entered it. What were you, child? A rock? A wind? Or perhaps a descending angel? No matter. You saved him and with great eloquence."

But Auguste appeared not to hear. He was gesturing almost frantically with his hands, pointing first to himself, then toward the mirror, and last, at Monsieur Hilaire.

"What are you trying to tell me, *mon petit?*"

The boy halted in thought. Then, this time quietly, he rose on his toes as tall as he could, assumed a kind of graveness, sucked in his cheeks to hollowness, and began to turn in a circle. With the same calm he became his own size and imitated himself. Then he pointed once more at himself and at the old man, but now at their reflections in the mirror.

"I understand! You want me to teach you."

The boy's two hands joined flat together in front of him and his eyes were very alive.

"You are willing to work? To work very hard? Remember that you must go on with your life on the farm. My years are as limited as my income. I cannot risk taking you in, for your own sake, and you might not have the force to endure two lives."

The boy did not stir from his plea.

"Could you come in the evenings? At first dusk? That way Madame Fer need not know and her ignorance would be a protection for you."

The boy nodded, just once.

The old man glanced down at his arthritically twisted fingers. He felt the pain that was a familiar inhabitant of his joints. Then he looked again at the eagerness before him. "Well, we can try," he said. "We can certainly try."

A quick gaiety livened his voice. "But this is an occasion! Let us toast the contract with a glass of wine."

A few moments later, as they clinked glasses, there was a brightness between them that did not come from the lamps or the fire. And they bowed to each other before they drank.

❧ *Two* ❧

And so it was the next day, at the first tide of evening, that a very small knock on the glass door began the apprenticeship.

"It is less than warm in this house," said Monsieur Hilaire, "but take off the hindrance of your jacket anyway. First come the exercises. Without them we are nothing."

At the word "we" the boy's face took on an unbelieving expression that was slightly streaked with joy.

"Every day, for the rest of your career, be it brief or long, the exercises. Now. Watch me and follow. When we come to the leaps you will have to provide the height. My own springs are too rusty to take me into the air."

First the head, then the arms, the torso, the legs, the feet; the progression of movements that limbered and stretched and strengthened. When Monsieur Hilaire was certain Auguste had memorized them, he signaled for a halt.

"Let us rest a few minutes. I have observed several

things about you." He smiled. The boy shrugged as though his back were burdened. "But why do you expect them to be bad?

"You are quick to learn, you are able to instruct your intelligence into your body. But you are full of corners. You angle yourself as though to ward off hurtfulness."

Auguste involuntarily clasped his right shoulder.

Monsieur Hilaire gazed past the boy and into the now blank dark of the night. "Did she beat you when you returned to the farm?"

Auguste's head lowered.

"I see. Also that you are no stranger to the stick. That accounts for your inability to go freely into space and that is something I cannot teach you. You must break that web yourself. But there is one gift that will aid you: imagination. You need not be a prisoner in that landscape."

The old man tossed Auguste's jacket to him. "Enough of philosophizing. Put on the soup—I made it from potatoes and cream—and we'll sit down to our after-theater supper."

The boy ate slowly as though each steaming spoonful was a thought, to be savored and digested. Monsieur Hilaire did not interrupt his inner dialogues, and for a time went into his own dreaming.

It was late when they finished and Auguste had washed the bowls and thrown the breadcrumbs out the back door for the morning birds as Monsieur Hilaire had instructed him. But in spite of the weariness that channeled his muscles, the old man delayed the boy's going.

"Let me say right out so that you won't ever wonder

why not, that I regret I cannot take you into my household. If I had ten more years of tomorrows, I would. That long would see you grown and ready. But I haven't. Nor have I any more money than will feed me until I go. So you would have no security to keep you safe when I become absent."

He paused as the boy made a question with his eyebrows.

"Are you puzzled by my using the word 'safe'?"

Auguste nodded and he watched Monsieur Hilaire's mouth forming the words as intently as he listened.

"Think back—back to all the shadows of your childhood, to Madame Fer's brutalities, to whatever cruelties were inflicted on you at the school, to all the stories and superstitions you may have heard in the village. These people you have known are no worse than the others that walk the world but they share with the others a common enemy, and that enemy is anyone who is different. They fear the boy who can't speak, the woman who lives by herself and believes in the curative powers of herbs, the man who reads books instead of going to the café at night, the person like me who has lived in the distant differentness of the theater. They are not willing to try to understand, so they react against them and occasionally do them injury. I say all this to warn you. Keep our lessons secret. If you don't you will be punished for them."

The boy's eyes changed into a kind of new tenderness and he tentatively reached out and touched the old man's sleeve.

Monsieur Hilaire smiled. "There is comfort in you," he said. Then he grew grave again. "Once I went into the café to buy my weekly bottles of wine and I overheard some talk between the Mayor and Madame Cresson, the pharmacist's wife. They are neither of them unintelligent but Madame was pondering the possibility of my being a wizard! I could only guess why. I had been foolish enough to practice that week in the unused meadow near the highway. She must have believed I was casting spells."

A small tremor shook him. Then he laughed. "And so I did, not so very long ago. And the next time you come I'll show you some pictures of what goes on inside a theater and how a stage is better than a meadow."

Ten minutes later, lying on his pallet in a corner of Madame Fer's barn, his blankets pulled high up over his ears, Auguste hoped to dream of flying. He already knew a few of the motions of flight. What kind of a bird, he wondered drowsily, would he be? The cow next to him stirred her hoofs in the straw. Auguste thrust one arm into the fragrant chill and patted her leg. A low moo introduced him to sleep.

So it went for the next round of days until almost a month was done. Each evening, his chores finished, his supper at Madame Fer's table hastily gulped, her grunted *bonne nuit* the only words spoken, he pretended to head for the stable and then, noiselessly, cut around the rear and through the woods to his teacher's house. He did not forget the warning, but it became a part of the background and he would have been a very surprised witness to a conversation, one Sunday morning, in the village café.

It was Madame Fer's custom, after two hours of loud bargaining for her week's provisions, to relax over an apéritif and collect the current gossip. This day she was greeted, as always, by the proprietor and his wife, with great cordiality. Then she sought out the most important man in the village, the Mayor, who immediately offered her a chair at his table and whatever refreshment was her pleasure.

She sipped so daintily at the rim of the goblet no one would have believed her raucous shouts of a few moments before over the price of the cabbages, or the measuring of the beans.

"You are looking most prosperous, monsieur," she said to the Mayor.

"I thank you, madame, for the compliment, but these are precarious times for us farmholders."

The thick woman dropped her eyelids. The Mayor was by far the wealthiest landowner in the district and his worries were completely verbal.

"And you, *chère* madame. All goes well?"

"I have my troubles," she replied.

"Alas, so have we all!" was his rejoinder. He had caught the signal. She had something to tell him.

"Some less than others, if I may say so," she said a little acidly.

"Indeed? But you have such courage, madame, a courage we all recognize. It is not every woman without a husband, God rest him, who can squeeze a profit from a farm virtually by herself." The Mayor waited.

Madame Fer's mood was now as sugared as the drink in her hand. "It's that boy," she said and paused.

"The mute? But what worry could he possibly represent? I've always believed you kept him firmly in hand. Not," he added hastily, "that a beating ever taught anything but good. Even my Gustave is disciplined when he needs it."

Madame Fer did not welcome this diversion to the Mayor's thirteen-year-old son, generally considered to be less than bright. "Auguste has changed," she said firmly.

"You mean he speaks?" exclaimed the Mayor.

The woman's laughter was so gusty all heads turned to stare. "More likely my well is filled with gold pieces!" she sputtered out.

Madame Cresson, the wife of the pharmacist, slipped a chair between the two and sat in it. "I heard what you said, Lucie. Is he worse? Has he taken to having fits?"

Madame Fer sobered. "No, not that." She was aware of the entire attention of the café. "It's even stranger." She paused for effect. The Mayor even had time to blow his nose. "He's happy."

Madame Cresson snorted. "And that's news? *Mon dieu*, what a brouhaha over nothing!"

The others watched Madame Fer begin to swell with resentment. "Nothing, is it? I guess you don't know what it is to extend Christian charity to a dummy and never a gesture of thanks or a smile or a little service done because of affection! Like living with a beast, an ailing sheep, or a two-legged dog. And then I catch him grinning at the wall, like he was at the cinema seeing something funny. Or the morning he was waltzing with the stable cat. And still never a sign toward me, a hint that I'm alive." She was silent a moment, her mental efforts creasing her broad face. "He's full of secrets, that's what it is! Secrets!"

The Mayor patted her arm. "Now, now, dear lady, it's very simple, after all."

The pharmacist's wife nodded.

A voice from the bar expressed the opinion for all of them. "The boy's gone potty!"

"Exactly," said the Mayor, "though I might have chosen more educated terms."

"But he's always been that!" protested Madame Fer.

"Tell you what," suggested the Mayor, who enjoyed solving everything for everybody, given the opportunity. "Just see as little of him as possible. He eats at your table, is it not so? Well, put his meals in the barn. Does he sleep in the house?"

The woman merely gestured a negative. She was faintly ashamed of this, having four empty bedrooms upstairs.

"*Enfin!*" The Mayor slapped the table with the flats of both hands. "Tranquility is yours. See that he does his work, and for the rest ignore him."

24

For a few minutes they drank their wine without speech. Then Madame Cresson, with a sly look at her neighbor, said, "I wonder, nonetheless, what he knows that we don't."

The Mayor rapped his glass for a refill. "Nothing worth speaking of, certainly."

Two men at the other end of the room guffawed. "Even if he could!" one called.

"Not enough quiet around here," said the Mayor, thoroughly irritated.

"We have another weird one none of us hear from," said the laborer who had mocked the Mayor. "The old man at the lodge-house."

"Monsieur Hilaire?" The Mayor's voice assumed respect. "He was a very famous mime."

"Fat lot of good it brought him!" commented another man. "He's poorer than I am."

"And besides," enjoined Madame Cresson, "who knows for sure that all that about his performing is true? Anyone here ever seen him on the stage?"

There was no assent.

"Have you, Monsieur le Maire?" she dug in. "You've been to Paris oftener than any of us."

The Mayor counted once more the four times he had been in the capital, twice as a child, his honeymoon, and the last trip ten years ago to bury a relative. The world of the theater was blank to him but he would not admit this now, before these villagers.

"Not seen him, no. But there were billboards with his name on them." He knew no one would attack this lie or even guess it to be one. His acquaintance with the outside world and his superior wealth accounted for his prestige.

"Might have belonged to a circus," conceded Madame Cresson.

The subject was ready to dwindle to a stop for lack of interest, and would have, except for the disgruntlement of Madame Fer. She had been cheated of her drama. "Always have wondered if that old rumor was true or not about Monsieur le Mime."

Madame Cresson took her bait. "That he came here rich and hid his money in his house?"

The Mayor shrugged. "Who's to know?"

"Not till he dies, anyway," said another.

"And that won't be long from now," said Madame Cresson with relish.

"You have special information?" asked the Mayor.

"I am the pharmacist's wife, am I not?"

"Meaning?" said Madame Fer, her voice twanging with asperity.

"Well, in deepest confidence of course," said Madame Cresson clearly, "it is known to me that he takes a very potent drug against pain."

"Cancer?" murmured the Mayor, impressed.

The informant merely pursed her lips.

"Then we'll soon know if the treasure tale is true or not," said the laborer.

"How do you make that out?" asked his companion.

"The last testament will be published."

"But if it is secret and revealed to only one person?"

"Have another glass," was the reply. "He's just a poor old crust in patched pants."

26

The conversation among the two women and the Mayor became private again.

"And how is your daughter?" asked Madame Fer of the other.

"Better. Though she still has those fevers."

Madame Fer clucked her sympathy while thinking once again how lucky she was not to be burdened with a sickly little girl like Avril who would never pay her way in life, if indeed she lived long enough to have one.

And that same day, after dusk, someone else was thinking of Avril, remembering and imitating her tentative manner of walking. It was Auguste.

"Let me guess who and what you are," Monsieur Hilaire was saying.

The boy had seemed to instantaneously lose weight, to have become enfeebled. His hand, raised to his forehead, was more delicate, almost without muscle.

"You are a girl," said Monsieur Hilaire. "Young. About nine. And you are ill." He clapped his hands together. "You are Avril Cresson, the child in the village who looks like a wind-flower!"

Auguste reverted to himself and bowed as the old man had taught him when taking a curtain call.

"Very good, *mon élève*! You are beginning to be perceptive about people. Your animals have always showed promise but now you progress! Let us commence with definitions. You are ready to try them. Tonight you will hold imaginary boxes, big and middle-sized and little. Start with age three."

For the next hour the drill continued successfully until it finished with a giant lifting a square of marble.

27

Their supper was gay. "Do you realize," he said to the boy, "that since we first worked together winter has been translated into spring? And you also."

Auguste smiled with such sweetness that the old man looked away. How he hated to leave this new being, this young tree of such talent he shone with it. Would he, after his teacher left him, find a way to continue growing, to send out new branches of bloom and leaf and fruit, or would he be trapped in this village prison of poverty and prejudice?

Painfully, his back bent, Monsieur Hilaire got up and went to a bookcase. Reaching behind a row of books he drew out a long box covered with scuffed red velvet. "I have no substance to leave you, *mon petit*, no treasure but this." He held it between his long fingers as though to warm it.

Auguste's hands moved, palms flat against the air, protesting Monsieur Hilaire's words.

"No, you must listen! Soon—perhaps even within the next tomorrows—I will be gone, and though the communication between us will never cease, it will be a silent one." He opened the lid and slowly turned it toward Auguste. The boy's eyes widened, then blinked as though scorched. Upon the black lining of the box lay a medallion, a twelve-pointed circle of pure gold, and at its center was a sapphire and from out the blue depth of the stone a star.

"At my farewell performance," said the old man softly, "before the footlights were extinguished and the stage cooled, they presented me with this last honor. I give it to you now, before you have earned it, because I will not be there to applaud your ultimate triumph. Hide it, my child, hide it into safety, and when you arrive at the moment to accept it—and you will know when that moment comes, I promise you—listen to the silence and remember me."

Auguste stood, his shoulders back, his head held very high, and made a cradle of his hands. With like formality Monsieur Hilaire rose and placed the box within them. And when the boy looked down he could no longer see the star at the center of the sapphire for the tears that filled his eyes.

❧ *Three* ❧

From evening to evening Auguste saw distinctly the seepage of the old man's strength almost as though, with the presentation of the medallion, Monsieur Hilaire had also given his ability to move through the day. One night, after practice, he realized there was no supper ready.

The boy rummaged through the cupboard, found a half-loaf of stale bread, two apples, and a box of potatoes. He started to put a pot on to boil and reached for a knife to peel a potato for soup.

"No, my child, prepare nothing for me. I am filled with drowsiness and cannot eat. But take what you wish for yourself."

Auguste's appetite vanished but he bit small into one of the apples.

The old man lay down on the couch. "I am cold," he said.

The boy ran upstairs and returned with a blanket. He spread it carefully over the long, lean figure and then, after a second's hesitation, tucked in all the edges.

"Thank you," murmured Monsieur Hilaire, but his tone was so faraway Auguste wondered if he were mistaking him for someone else, someone loved long ago.

"Go now. It is time."

Auguste squatted on his heels and gazed at the narrow, scored face. He tried to will the deep eyes to open, to speak to him even if the breath could not carry the voice. But there was only complete stillness.

Then, as if the message had been received, the old man's left hand lifted, the fingers opened and bent a little backward. They were telling him to leave, they were ushering him out.

Auguste rose, and on tiptoe all the way, backed to the door. The hand fell. He grabbed the handle of the door and slid into the night. Then, suddenly, he began to race, across the terrace, through the woods and onto the road, and he didn't stop until he had flung himself, face down, onto his stable bed.

And when, the next afternoon, he went once more to the house, he knew it had happened. It did not need the long funeral car or the limousine waiting for the three tall men just outside the house to tell him.

But he came near enough to hear their words, as though just listening to them might even for these few moments hold back the fact.

"I regret," one of them was saying, "that I did not come last week, but Hercule never hinted at an emergency in his note."

"Nor to me," said another who looked like a prince.

"How very poor he was at the end!" the third said, sighing.

"But that was his choice," said the first. "What he saved he made over to the daughter of Madame Silvie, don't you remember?"

The others nodded.

Auguste suddenly felt so lonely he trembled. These men had made a stranger of his friend.

As he turned to go one of them called to him. "Who are you, little one? Did you wish to speak to Monsieur Hilaire?"

Auguste nodded, knowing no other way to respond.

"Alas, he died last night. Peacefully, we believe. We had come to take him back to Paris for a visit." The tall man paused and looked over the boy's head and down the road. "And so we shall," he added as if to himself. "You knew him well?"

Auguste nodded again.

"He was content here, wasn't he?" But when Auguste did not reply the man ignored him and continued speaking to the others. "A very rundown property. Won't bring much if it does sell."

At that moment two men whom Auguste recognized as the village morticians came from the house carrying the long box of new pine.

Auguste looked quickly at the closing door. Couldn't Monsieur Hilaire be standing there, this coffin and these men all a mistake? But as they slid the box into the hearse, the visitors climbed into the limousine and the last words from one of them were, "We will precede you. You have the address in Paris." And slowly, like storm shadows, they rolled down the road and out of sight.

For a long time Auguste stood, staring at the façade of the unlighted house. No tears came to his eyes. No heaviness weighted him. Instead, from out of this new stillness, from beyond this new aloneness, rose a kind of fire in him, a reed of warmth no wider than a grass blade, and with it a deeper kind of breathing started within him. It moved him around the house and to the rear window, where first he had seen Hercule Hilaire. He looked inside. He made his farewell. With no sound at all he brought his hands together three times. Then he turned about-face and ran swiftly into the woods just beyond the terrace, and when he had arrived at a clearing he began his daily exercises.

So it went for a week: the usual early rising, the long day of farm chores, the hurriedly swallowed soup and bread, then the retreat to his corner of the barn, and when Madame Fer had fastened the shutters and latched the front door, herself inside, off to his space of meadow in the concealment of trees. There was no lessening

of the small flame, the desire to train his body to obey his imagination, and he had even found a long strip of sheet metal in the village dumping grounds that he nailed against a tree trunk and used for a mirror. It was true that his image was watery and too wide a movement cut off his reflection at both edges, but the prop reassured him, kept his efforts real. And sometimes he smiled as he balanced on an invisible tightrope or mounted a ladder that wasn't there as though Monsieur Hilaire were standing just to the right of the clearing, speaking his approval.

But at the end of that first week, on Sunday, just as the first slackening of light dimmed the grass and charcoaled the trees, and Auguste was ready to try being a crow in a wheat field, he heard a clot of hushed voices coming from the back of the house. He crept toward the sounds, keeping as low as possible until he halted behind the hedge of the terrace.

Three boys were crouched at the window where Auguste had first glimpsed Monsieur Hilaire, peering in.

"The place is sealed, I tell you!" said the largest whom Auguste recognized to be Gustave, the son of the Mayor. Auguste grimaced. This was the town bully who had cornered him day after day in the schoolyard, commanding him to talk.

"So it is sealed!" answered a smaller boy with a face like a razor. "That doesn't mean we can't get in."

"You afraid or something?" demanded the third of Gustave.

"Me, afraid? You crazy?"

"Well, you act like it. You talk up the treasure the old man left and now you want to back out!"

"Oh, shut up, Jean. He's with us, isn't he?"

Gustave stood erect. "Tell you what. I'll go find a rock by the road and we can crash a pane of this door and get in."

"Good," assented the others. "Meanwhile we'll inspect the front."

"Meet you here in five minutes."

Auguste suddenly wished he were a monster, a dragon, a lion, anything with teeth and claws savage enough to strip the skin from these marauders' backs. They had no right here. They were an insult to all the hours this house had sheltered his teacher, all the sunrises and sunsets that had touched this roof and pleased Monsieur Hilaire. But what could he do, a person with not even half the strength of Gustave, much less the two others?

He glanced down at his hands, helplessly, and then their whiteness in the blueing air gave him an idea. He arrowed so fast across the field to the road he seemed to be flying, and in three minutes he was in the stable, ripping off the muslin sheet that covered his straw pallet. Bundling it in his arms he flashed back the way he had come.

He arrived at his hiding place just as Gustave returned, slowly, from his search.

"Got it," the boy said, holding up a pointed fragment of stone.

"Then get to it!" ordered Jean.

"Who's the boss around here?" said Gustave, blustering.

"Nobody," replied the smallest, but he stepped beyond Gustave's reach.

"You want a beating?" said the bully, made confident by the retreat.

"What the devil!" exclaimed Jean. "Are we here to argue or find that treasure? We stay here too late and they're going to miss us at home. Give me that rock. I'll do it."

But just as he raised his arm something whished past his cheek. "What the damnation was that?"

The other two were startled, then the little one laughed jerkily. "It's only a branch of leaves!"

"But where did it come from? Somebody had to throw it!" Gustave's voice was high now.

"Oh, don't be an old biddy!" scolded Jean. "Maybe a vampire flew by."

"You shut your mouth!" ordered Gustave. "No telling what's in this house. Maybe—maybe—"

"Yes?" urged the small one in a whisper. "Maybe what?"

"Ghosts, that's what he means!" said Jean scornfully. "Maybe this wreck is haunted. Maybe the old creep who lived here has got himself a sword and he's after your blood!" Once again he lifted his hand to crack open the windowpane.

At this instant Auguste, the sheet around him, held wide at arm's-length, leaped from behind the hedge, circled once, and disappeared around the corner of the terrace.

Three shrieks and a clatter, a sound of running, and a loud thump disrupted the silence of the night.

Auguste peeked past the angle of the house. Jean and the little one were gone. Gustave was sprawled on the

pavement, both hands clutching his ankle, his mouth rounded for a roar. Instead he began to sob.

Auguste heaved with silent laughter as he folded the sheet and went toward his former enemy.

He stationed himself in quietness above him, relaxed and tall.

Gustave looked up. The fear left his face and was replaced by astonishment. "You?" he stammered. "The dummy?"

Auguste merely smiled and somehow this smile acted as a control over the other.

Gustave's voice was almost meek when he spoke again. "Didn't know you knew the old man. You live here, now he's dead?"

Auguste's smile did not change.

"None of my business, I guess." He looked away, thoroughly uncomfortable before this concentration. "Twisted my ankle when I fell," he continued. Then he raised his head. "Would you help me up?"

The next moment was a long one. Then Auguste replied by holding out both his hands and braced himself to pull. Gustave grasped the hands and together they got him up. He tried his injured foot. He limped a few steps, testing. "At least it's not broken," he said and wiped the few tears from his cheeks. "You're an odd one, all right. Not just because you can't talk, either." He half-turned. "Well, guess I'll be going. Thanks for giving me a hoist." Once more he paused. Then he went forward, his shoulders slumped. An involuntary gasp accompanied his third step.

Auguste moved to his side, pulled Gustave's arm

across his own shoulders, and took half his weight onto himself. Very carefully they maneuvered themselves around the house and to the road. Here it was easier. And when they had gone a hundred yards and had adjusted to the awkward gait, Gustave looked sideways at his rescuer and suddenly smiled. "You made one hell of a fine ghost!" he said, and seeing the grin curve Auguste's face entirely upward, he burst into laughter loud enough for both of them.

❧ *Four* ❧

Two mornings later, so early the sun was still red and rising, Auguste, in the far pasture with the cows, heard his name, small and shrieked. It was still an hour to breakfast and Madame Fer never varied her routine so as not to lose a moment of Auguste's work time. He made a running jump over the one calf, pretending to be a cow-bird, and then fell into a trot toward the house.

She was poised in the doorway, her arms crossed. "I called you twice!"

He waited, his eyes on her shoes, for the usual lengthy tirade.

Instead she spoke to someone behind her. "See what I mean? His silence is impertinent! And I am certain that what he is thinking would crisp an angel. Well? Come in and eat!"

As he entered the bare room he saw Madame Cresson seated by the fire, her coat still on, her cheeks pink as though she had hurried.

"It's not easy to live with a creature who can't even

give you a 'good morning.' Get that porridge inside you, and no dawdling. I want to lock up before I leave. Won't be back until the Lord knows when."

The pharmacist's wife took over with a gusty sigh. "Perhaps she'll improve before the day's end."

"One hopes so," said Madame Fer gloomily. "But the child has always been fragile."

"Yes, Avril is like a butterfly, my husband always says," said the mother, "and perhaps she is destined only for a brief life." She took out her handkerchief.

The farm woman patted her clumsily on the back. "No need to take on this soon. Trouble is you've been alone with this responsibility too long. Company's what you need during the watch." She coiled a fat brown shawl over her shoulders. "Finished, have you?" She swept the bowl from the table and placed it in the sink, then thrust a heel of bread at Auguste. "If I'm very late getting back, you just fend for yourself." She propelled Madame Cresson and Auguste outdoors and secured the lock. She did not glance at the boy again but led the way down the road, the other woman three steps behind and pushing herself to keep up.

For the next few hours Auguste worked at high speed in order to extend his freedom at the end of the day. But when he sat down at ease against a fencepost near the front gate to eat his bread he saw, almost within reach, a green and blue spotted butterfly. It alighted on a stem of milkweed. Its wings fluttered for an instant, then stilled. Auguste stopped chewing. A kind of immense pause descended over the meadow as though a signal had been received by every beetle and bird and stir of

air. Then, as though possessed of an inner, finite whirlwind, the butterfly revived, shot into space and then, wildly faltering, its wings now a shudder of colors, dropped to the ground.

Auguste felt himself held by this tiny death. His hands trembled a little. He stuffed the bread into his jacket pocket and very slowly touched his palms together and watched them become wings. They were remembering the drama. At last they ceased. Auguste wiped the perspiration from his forehead and the words of the woman came back to him. "Avril is like a butterfly." He took a deep breath and got up. If she were dying as Monsieur Hilaire had died then she would be going to the same place, to the same blurred landscape of light and music and bright wings. Maybe she would take a message. For the first time since his teacher's absence he felt joy, and without hesitating strode down the highroad.

Auguste knew that he must not be seen. Any one of the village people would report his coming to Madame Fer, and for punishment she might lock him up in the barn. This had happened once when he was six and only the sweet smell of the cows had kept him from panic. He remembered where Avril lived. In the days when he had gone to school he had noticed where she turned in. The house was the largest, next to the Mayor's, two-storied, and constructed of wood instead of plaster. An oak tree shaded one side of it. Auguste entered the village by the alleys, and as fast as he could, clambered up into the concealment of the oak branches. Settling into a wide crotch, he looked and listened.

At first the voices from downstairs smeared together. Then as the other sounds, of dogs, a distant tractor, and the nearby birds sorted themselves, the words became audible.

Madame Cresson was speaking. "She's in a bad way. Won't eat, can't seem to sleep peacefully, thrashes around all night. I don't know. I just don't know."

Another woman spoke. It was Madame Fer. "No fever, you say?"

"Not this time. Just fades off, wispy-like. My husband and I can almost clock it. She gets very tired and pale as chalk. Then stops wanting to eat. Then takes to bed. Happened ever since she was a baby."

"Ever brought her to the capital to consult a specialist?"

"Long time ago. He said she needed the mountains.

Fresh air. But we live in the country. I never understood the sense of it and his fee was enormous, not counting the expense of the journey."

"Maybe you keep her too sheltered," Madame Fer suggested, an opinion she had held from the beginning. "Nothing like work for the young. Makes them sturdy."

The other woman's reply could not be heard, but Auguste thought there was weeping.

Then the mother's voice came from the open window immediately opposite his perch. It was almost whispered. "See how she lies? Avril? *Chérie?* Are you awake?"

A sound like a small owl in a chimney replied, "Yes, Maman."

"Madame Fer is here to see you. Will you try a cup of soup now?"

"No, thank you. Later, Maman."

"We'll leave you then, but remember your promise to eat."

Auguste heard the bedroom door shut, then the hushed chatter of the two women returning to the ground floor.

He lowered his body, hands around the branch, and swung himself back and forth three times. On the third swing his feet found the wide window sill and he let the motion carry him upward and against the window. For a second he stayed, flat as a silhouette, against the glass. But the girl in the bed had her head turned away. He angled himself inside and went to stand at the foot of her bed. The green, flower-sprigged coverlet accentuated her pallor. Her hair that reminded Auguste of autumn sunlight was tousled upon the pillow. The whole image had an underwater feeling and the boy recalled all the hours

45

he had spent on his stomach, his nose touching the surface of the stream, regarding the world below, himself a
fish.

But with a soft suddenness it changed. Avril opened
her eyes. Such a blue shone from the pallor of her face, it
was the sapphire of Monsieur Hilaire come to life. Two
of them.

"Who are you?" There was no fright in her tone, only
a kind of submerged wonderment.

Auguste bowed as though making an entrance. He
would become her court juggler, for surely this was a
queen. From his pockets he drew forth five imaginary
balls. One after the other they took to the air, circling
each other faster and faster. Auguste's hands never fal-
tered in their rhythm. Then, both arms outflung, he con-
signed them to vanishment and plucked from nowhere
two hoops. First he whirled them on both arms, then
jumped into them and twirled them on one leg, dancing
on the other. These, too, were discarded. Last he
squatted on the floor, his legs and arms folded tight
around him. Avril could only see the top of his head. She
sat up to watch. For a moment he remained enclosed.
What was he? A seed? Then slowly, slowly he began to
rise, to unfold until he stood upright and his hands were
leaves and his head a flower. For five seconds he held
the magic. Then relaxed into himself.

A clapping, a weak effort at applause, cued him into a
low bow. And when he faced the girl again he was smiling.

"Oh! Oh!" was all she could seem to say. Then a smile
as real as the color of her eyes covered her face and her

cheeks pinked. "I do know you! I do! You're Auguste, the boy who can't talk. Oh, that was—that was like a fairy tale! Thank you!"

Auguste turned to leave. Soon now her mother would be coming back.

"Don't go! Please!"

He shook his head, but as he put one leg over the window sill he gestured first to her and then to himself and Avril knew what he meant. She must find him. She nodded. "I will, just as soon as I can."

He placed his forefinger to his mouth.

"I know. I mustn't tell."

She watched him fling himself onto the nearest branch and then the leaves covered him. And when her mother came next to observe her the woman cried out, "But what has happened, *chérie*? You are sitting up! Madame Fer, come look! There has been a miracle!"

Avril merely smiled. "Maman, could I have that soup now? And maybe a piece of toast?"

Madame Cresson's hands flew upward. "Did you hear that? She asked for toast with her soup! And tomorrow a nice little cutlet with mashed potatoes and perhaps an omelette for supper and—" She gabbled happily all the way to the kitchen where Madame Fer awaited her.

"What happened?"

"What indeed! I'll question the child later but now she's going to eat again!" She began to cry but did not pause in her preparations, sniffling over the pot as though it were filled with sliced onions.

Ten minutes later both she and Madame Fer were witnesses to the hunger of her daughter. And when she had spooned up the last mouthful and was leaning back against her raised pillows, Madame Cresson led the questions.

"Don't be alarmed, *chérie*, if I ask you something quite odd," said her mother.

Avril smiled. What could have been odder than the magical visit of Auguste, the sad, twisted boy she had never bothered with when he went to school. But now he was different, as though he had gone ahead of her, gone on a journey she could not even imagine.

"Can you believe it?" murmured Madame Fer. "She's well!"

"What did you want to say, Maman?"

"While we were downstairs, did anyone come to see you? A vision of someone, like a dream or—?" Her words faded.

"You mean a guardian angel—something like that?"

"God be praised! It *is* a miracle!" gasped Madame Fer. "Just wait till the village hears about this!"

"Did it have a halo?" continued her mother. "Tell me!"

"No halo, no wings," said Avril, suppressing the urge to reveal the truth.

"A dream," Madame Fer stated flatly.

"A dream," echoed the other. She hugged her daughter for the fifth time. "A dream from heaven! And that's as good as an angel."

Avril could not resist one hint. "He was a juggler."

Both women laughed. "That settles it. Pure invention. But come now, Madame Fer, we're going to celebrate with a glass of my cherry brandy. You rest, child, and I must also get the news to your father. He will be so happy!"

And so he was, although like the rest of the villagers he remained puzzled. Avril was up and outdoors in three days and for a week she was trailed by comments of

"There's the little one who rose from the dead." Avril did not vary her replies to their curiosity and it was not until she was back in school that she, one recess, went further.

She and the Mayor's son were splitting an apple.

"There's a lot of gossip about you," said Gustave, taking the larger half. "Know what I think?"

"What?" Avril had never liked this oversized, arrogant boy.

"That someone really did come into your room."

"What makes you think that?"

"I'll tell you if you promise to keep it a secret."

"I promise."

Gustave recounted his raid on the house of Monsieur Hilaire, how Auguste had very effectively appeared as a ghost, and that only he knew the truth of it. He had never let the other two boys in on the facts. They still believed the ghost to be real. "He could have pushed me down and stomped on me if he'd wanted to. Keep wondering why he didn't. He's a good one," he concluded.

Avril was looking at Gustave with warmth. "Maybe you are too," she said.

Gustave shoved his hands in his pockets. "You seen him since?" he asked to ride out his embarrassment.

"No, but I'm going this afternoon. It's a long walk but I can make it now."

"Can I go with you?"

"No. Next time. I want to thank him alone."

Gustave nodded. "Next time, then. Say *bonjour* for me."

But Avril was never given the chance. She found him

in the barn, raking hay from the loft. He bowed to her from above. She bowed to him and then they both grinned. He flew down the ladder like a monkey and then hopped before her, swinging an invisible tail. She laughed aloud.

"Oh, Auguste!" she said, "I never knew there were people like you! I mean, all my life has been so solemn. They never let me do anything or go anywhere, even on the church picnics. I'm like a trained poodle on a short leash. But when I saw you juggling all those beautiful things, somehow I could see them better than even my parents' faces and I wanted to be where you are."

The boy's eyes were suddenly grave. He pointed upward and then traced, with an expansive gesture, the shape of a crescent. Then, as though the ascent were very perilous, he slowly began to climb a rope, hand over hand, his feet never leaving the ground, yet Avril saw him go so high she almost lost sight of him. He came down carrying something that he cradled, and standing before her once more, he presented her with the new moon.

At that very instant there was a yell from the yard. "Avril, you come out of there! You've no business with that boy!"

Madame Fer seized the girl by the sleeve and pulled her to the doorway. "No telling what he thinks or does. May be plotting a murder for all I know! Your mother know you're here?" She shook her but not too hard.

"No, madame."

"You ever do this again and I'll tell her. Understood?"

Avril nodded. Had she gotten Auguste into more trou-

ble than his ordinary existence? She wished, for his sake, she had never come. But what was he doing? He had squatted on his heels, his back to both of them, and seemed to be writing in the dirt.

"You see what a little animal he is? Can't even pretend politeness."

Avril drew herself from the woman's grip. With a dignity that surprised Madame Fer into allowing it, she said, "I will say goodbye to Auguste before I go," and stopped in front of him. She took one rapid glance at what he had traced in the dust, saw it was a map with a house on it and over the roof was a half-moon. She recognized the house. It had belonged to the old man who had died a few weeks ago.

"Goodbye, Auguste, and thank you again."

She tapped the map with her toe. He did not look up.

"Good day, madame," she said to the farm woman and walked down the road.

They had understood one another. That evening, an hour before Avril was due home for supper, she discovered the boy waiting for her in front of Monsieur Hilaire's hedge. He led her to the terrace at the rear.

She began their conversation at its break. "I truly thought I held the moon," she said.

He smiled like laughter.

"Do you live here now?"

He shook his head.

"But you come every day? What for?"

He beckoned her to follow and guided her to the clearing. He demonstrated a set of exercises before the metal strip.

"Oh!" said Avril, drawing out the sound. "Was he your teacher? Are you going to be a mime too?"

Auguste crossed his fingers and held them aloft like tiny torches.

"And no one knows but me?"

He nodded.

"Then we are friends," she said and ran to him and kissed him on both cheeks. He did not respond but stood as if stunned.

"We are," she said for both of them. "But you have to get used to me. I must go now but I will come whenever I can at this hour to this place." With a wave of her hand she turned and ran, but for the next few moments Auguste stayed, staring as though she were still there.

❧ *Five* ❧

Each day for the next two weeks seemed to ripen for Auguste with the same pace as the countryside. The new green of spring had changed to the permanent shades of summer. The cabbages were solid rounds, the carrot tops high and frothy in the vegetable plots. The first roses roped the fences red and white and yellow, and their fragrances columned above the walls of the village gardens.

His farm tasks done, he walked through the late afternoon to his teacher's house, sometimes delaying his arrival to anticipate his delight. For almost every evening Avril was there. She did not speak to him until he had completed his daily exercises. Then, for a few minutes, they talked, about anything.

"I've never known any animals except a few dogs and cats and never one of my own."

The boy grinned, and humping his back, his hands before him like rodent's paws, his head quick, he became a squirrel. Or a goose. Or a hen with her brood.

One of Avril's favorites was the turkey, and her giggles usually shattered the interpretation with Auguste rolling on the grass in silent laughter.

And she told him, this strange boy who understood with his eyes, things she had never tried to word before. Things about her parents, how they had chained her to illness, kept her indoors away from friends, forbidden her to go to parties where she might be infected with germs, and how very lonely she had become until even her private thoughts were rags without color or shape or interest. They had not expected her to live to maturity and she had accepted this judgement, not really caring, until—and here she seemed to take on the full bloom of a rose—until Auguste showed her what magic was.

In reply, when she had finished and the first drift of evening had hushed even the birds in the trees, Auguste got up into another self and began to dance. It was not patterned directly from a person or an animal or a plant, but part of all of them, a kind of spirit that made them grow, that watched over them, that was their secret partner. His movements were slow and wide and encircling and when he was done his breath was shallow and he fell as if exhausted onto the thick grass.

A long moment later Avril spoke, very softly. "I wish," she said, "I wish Monsieur Hilaire might have seen that."

Auguste looked at her from very far away and only nodded.

It was the next afternoon that Avril brought Gustave with her.

She greeted Auguste nervously. "He asked, Auguste.

He asked to come with me."

He wavered, ghostlike, in front of the visitor.

Gustave laughed. "I never had such a scare in my whole life!"

"What scare?" asked Avril, though she had heard the story before, seating herself gracefully on the grass. She was playing queen to her two courtiers today. Since meeting Auguste she inhabited many other people than the sickly shell she had broken out of.

"You act it and I'll tell it," said Gustave, dropping down beside Avril, quite unaware of her royalty. So as he described the invasion of the three boys, Auguste filled out his sentences with movement, even to becoming all three of them. His imitation of Gustave sent Avril into the giggles. Her imaginary crown fell off.

The small silence at the end of the play was a shared one. Gustave chewed on a grass blade, Avril hummed under her breath, and Auguste stood as though waiting for something. It came from Avril. "Auguste, what was Monsieur Hilaire like? He only came into the village once a week and then very early."

"Mostly they made fun of him," added Gustave.

"I wonder why," murmured the girl.

"Because he was different, I guess," said Gustave.

"You mean he didn't belong here? I'm different from you and you from me. But nobody sniggers at us."

"Oh, I don't know, Avril," said Gustave. "I'm not too bright about people. But take Auguste, for instance. They gossip about him, even say he's odd in the head. Not to be trusted."

Avril snorted, court manners forgotten. "What fools! I never had any fun at all until we became friends, Auguste and I. And you—why he changed you from being a lump to somebody I can talk to!"

"Don't get angry!" Gustave protested. "I'm just re-

peating what I hear. Needn't think I agree with them."
He turned to Auguste to divert Avril's misdirected in-
dignation. "Do tell us about the old man. He was on the
stage, wasn't he?"

The still look Auguste gave to each of them lasted so
long they felt molded into it. Then he broke it with a
smile. He gestured to Avril to follow him and ran into
the forest. In three minutes they were back, Auguste
holding something in both hands that was shaped like a
jewel box of red velvet.

He placed it with tenderness on the ledge of the stone
terrace then turned to his audience, suddenly older and
taller and someone else. He reached for the box, drew
out the medallion, and then, as if his hands belonged to
another person, drew it over his head and let it hang on
his chest. He was Monsieur Hilaire accepting it.

Avril let out her breath in a sigh. "Oh, how very beautiful! He was decorated. How famous he must have
been!"

Auguste quickly took it off and tucked it back into its
silken nest.

"And he gave it to you?" said Gustave almost unbe-
lievingly. "Better hide it well," he continued.

Auguste nodded.

Gustave got to his feet. "I must start back now. But
thank you for letting me stay. Say, Auguste, tomorrow's
Sunday and I know you come to the market with Madame Fer. How about dropping by my house when she
goes to the café? Avril, too. I haven't any treasures like
that one but—" His voice wisped off as if he expected a
refusal.

"Want to?" Avril asked of Auguste. The boy nodded eagerly. "All right, we'll be there." Avril had resumed her queenship. "Now you can take me home."

When the two were out of sight Auguste stroked the box with a forefinger then arrowed off to its hiding place that was under a chestnut tree.

❧ *Six* ❧

"I'm tired to the bone!" wheezed Madame Fer as she sat down in her usual chair in the café.

"It's this unseasonable weather," suggested the Mayor, beckoning to the serving boy.

"Maybe," Madame Cresson joined in. "Or something more than just too much sun."

"Meaning?" Madame Fer was ready for any maliciousness.

The pharmacist's wife smoothed her tight dress. She hesitated. "Avril, my very own daughter, that's what! She's just not normal."

The Mayor's eyebrows raised to his hairline. "Why madame, she looks healthy as a young hen! And for the first time in her life!"

"Exactly!" Madame Cresson pursed her lips. "Why now? Never has before. My husband and I have sat up a thousand nights with the child, counting her breaths. We've suffered over her as we might have over ten others."

"And you're complaining?" persisted the Mayor.

"No. I'm frightened."

Madame Fer let out a loud "Zut!" her hands upflung.

"She goes off to play after school and comes back singing or sometimes laughing or pretending things to herself, only she won't tell us what."

"She's turned peculiar, you mean?" asked Madame Fer.

The other woman's head bobbed decisively.

The Mayor burst into guffaws. "Women's talk! She and my son have become good friends and the Lord knows he's sensible enough. Often wonder if he isn't a trifle backward."

"And you think that isn't unusual?" said Madame Cresson, attacked and now attacking. "Gustave was the tyrant of the school—don't deny it!—until lately. Now he's the little gentleman. Why? I tell you all, there's something loose in this village, something we should beware of!"

At that instant a hoarse shout exploded outside the café.

The ten people in the café poured out the door, the Mayor in the lead.

Three streets to the right, at the edge of the village, stood a large, barrel-chested yellow dog, braced in a quivering stance of fear against the semicircle that surrounded him. A man threw a stick at him. The dog growled, then barked, his teeth showing white, saliva dripping from his jaws.

"Mad dog! Mad dog!"

"Look at him! He's frothing at the mouth!"

"Get a gun somebody!"

"Kill him!"

By this time all the houses had emptied. Even the smallest children were part of the compact crowd senselessly screeching with the rest.

The Mayor spied his son. "Gustave!" he called. "Bring my rifle immediately!"

But before the boy had a chance to turn back someone stepped in front of him, someone in a tattered jacket, his arms up as if to halt the whole town, making no sound. And as he ran toward the frantic hound a like silence fell over the villagers.

A yard away, Auguste slid to a stop. His arms now at his sides, he faced the dog in a stillness so intense that later one witness swore they had spoken to each other, animal to human. The barking lowered to snarls. Then the boy slowly spread his legs and began to sidestep around the dog. The dog swiveled to confront him until his rear was to the crowd. Holding fast to the concentration that was like a leash between them, Auguste moved backward, foot by foot. The animal followed. The snarling had ceased.

Just as they reached the boundary of the last street, Auguste broke into a trot and swerved around the corner and out of sight. The dog leaped after him.

The silence broke into a hundred exclamations.

"Did you see it? Did you?"

"Witchcraft!"

"Crazy as the dog!"

Only Gustave, and close behind Avril, cut out from the confusion and ran in the direction of their friend's disappearance. But though they searched every street and alley they could not find him.

"Let's go to the old man's house and wait there," said Avril.

Gustave nodded, his face set in gloom. "We may wait forever," he muttered, and as they walked through the dispersing people he never even noticed his father addressing the lingerers, instructing them to keep their guns ready to shoot the hound on sight.

It was half an hour later in the dark of a tool shed when Auguste loosened his grip from around the jaws of the dog and began to stroke his throat. He seemed to be choking on something. His breath hacked irregularly in a kind of smothered cough. The dog was lying on his side now and his legs jerked spasmodically. Very gently Auguste pried his mouth open. The animal winced. The boy saw the reason for his madness. A burr was fastened onto his tongue at the entrance to his throat. With the quickness of a bird, Auguste's fingers plucked it out. The dog gagged once and then, sniffing the boy's hand, licked it, all over. Auguste leaned down and placed his cheek lightly on the dog's flank. The two of them rested together.

It was very late, the moon already halfway high, when they arrived at Monsieur Hilaire's house. Avril had left but Gustave still sat on the terrace wall with no hope in him, only a wish. When he saw the shadowlike boy and dog approach he let out a whoop. "You're here! You're here!" He pounded Auguste's shoulders, then remembered the dog.

Auguste grinned and led the hound up to Gustave. His tail stiffened, then wagged.

"Am I happy to see you! Avril had to go but I'll give

her the good news on my way home. She was afraid they might suspect about our meetings. I'll get no worse than a hiding for being late. You going to keep the dog here? His life won't be worth a *centime* in the village. Some idiot will kill him." He was chattering in his relief. "Tell you what. Avril and I will bring him food every day. You'll have to keep out of sight too for a while. This was all they needed to convince themselves you're a—" He cut off his last word.

Auguste put his hands behind his head and crooked his forefingers into horns.

Gustave laughed. "That's right! A devil."

⚘ *Seven* ⚘

For the next three weeks it was as though a kind of noonday darkness were seeping through the atmosphere of the village. It spread to the farms. Great, gray clouds moved across the blazing sun but released no rain. And the comments in the village café became more and more unreasoning.

It was a farmer who cued up the final curtain on that third Sunday. Contrary to custom, he had already had so much to drink his speech slurred. "I lost them, three of them, yesterday. Had to slaughter."

All other conversation stopped.

"Slaughter what?" asked the Mayor, wiping the moisture from his jowls.

"My three prize pigs, of course!" said the farmer.

Several clicked their tongues sympathetically. "Troubles all over," said another. "Five of my cows are giving sour milk and some none at all."

"You should hear my wife carry on about the fall off in eggs," said a third. "First time in years. She crosses herself every time she goes into the coop."

"And my corn's wizened past being any use as feed."

Madame Cresson looked toward the Mayor. He sat silent. She spoke. "Any good news from your house?" They all knew that his son, Gustave, had caught the summer grippe only the week before, but the pharmacist's wife had been informed by her husband that the boy was not responding to the medicines given him.

The Mayor heaved to his feet and walked to the door as though he had arrived at exhaustion. "Got to get back," was all he said, looking at no one.

"Bad, is he?" questioned Madame Fer.

Madame Cresson gave her report, finishing with, "It's my opinion they're afraid of the outcome."

"How is that possible?" the café's proprietor broke in. "The boy's heftier than a mule."

Madame Cresson sniffed. "Gone into a delerium, he has. Keeps calling for that bastard boy who lives with you." She had turned to Madame Fer.

"Whatever for?" Madame Fer retorted. "Auguste left school because Gustave tormented the sense out of him. No kind feelings between those two!"

"I'm only telling what I know. Heard him myself. Boy doesn't even open his eyes, just keeps asking. Something about a dog, too."

"Maybe," one of the men offered, "maybe that mad dog bit him. Never did find the creature. Just vanished."

Then Madame Fer spoke for all of them. "Don't like any of it. People and animals sickening for no reason. Rain holding off as though it were warned away. Streams drying up. Dust so dense you sink in it up to the ankles. And even our Mayor's not acting like himself, seems to have forgotten he's the leader of the village."

"Well, his son is seriously ill," said the proprietor's wife.

"It's not that entirely, take my word for it," said Madame Fer sententiously. "It's what is poisoning us all. Something unseen, something evil has been welcomed into this village. And by whom?"

It did not need Madame Fer to speak the name. Their thought was single and together.

At that moment Avril and Auguste were hurrying down the road from the farmhouse. The girl had promised Gustave she would fetch his friend, though she wasn't certain the fevered, lost-eyed boy, so straight in his bed, had understood her.

"I don't know what's wrong with Gustave," Avril was saying. "It's like the time I was sent to my grandmother's by train. I didn't want to go exactly. I was afraid I'd throw up in public. But beyond that I loved the way she left me alone. I could get up when I pleased, read in bed at night, and just wander anywhere during the day. But until I got to her house I wasn't sure. So, anyway, when I was put in my seat by the window and the train doors were all shut and the wheels began to roll I wanted to cry out to someone, anybody, to help me—to get me off—but there wasn't anyone to hear."

Auguste took her hand and swung it in his for a few yards.

"Do you mind the truth, Auguste? About Gustave, I mean. Or, at least, it's what I believe."

She looked for his assent and received a smile that kept the rising tears out of her throat.

69

"I believe Gustave is dying. And I believe he wants to and doesn't want to."

Auguste pointed to himself.

"Yes. He's calling out to someone the way I was. Only he has you."

Suddenly a giant spurt of dust preceded them. It was the dog.

"Oh, Auguste! He's come untied! And now we haven't time to take him back!"

The hound danced around his master, his tongue lolling happily from one side of his jaws. Auguste slapped him lightly on one side but the animal was so filled with gaiety and freedom he merely barked once and raced ahead.

"You've never named him," said Avril to retard her sadness.

Auguste nodded and sketched an outline larger than himself in the air and changed his gait.

"You christened him 'Gustave'? Oh, he'll like that. We'll tell him."

But Avril never had the opportunity.

The instant the three of them entered the village the first person to see them cried out, "The dog's back! Clear the streets!" Instead, like flies upon carrion, there was an immediate gathering of people in front of and behind them.

"Get him!"

"Who has a gun?"

Before the café, just across from the Mayor's house, they were forced to halt.

"Run!" Avril ordered the dog. "Go home!"

But the first stone had been thrown and the dog cowered toward Auguste.

The noise increased to a kind of jagged howling, men's and women's voices tight and shrill, and the children shrieked, excited into senselessness.

An explosion shattered the screaming. The dog dropped like a sack of skin, his breath gone, his blood blackening the dust.

Auguste, his right hand clenched around Avril's left, did not pause. He walked the last ten feet to the door of the Mayor's house and raised his left hand to pull at the knocker.

No one spoke. No one stirred.

The door slowly opened and in the center of the dark threshold stood the Mayor. He might have been a hundred years old. His lips parted and mouthed words that did not sound. He tried again. They came. "My son is worse." He turned completely around and the door closed.

An angry rumbling, like a growl, issued from the crowd. The second stone flew forward, this time aimed at the boy. A third and a fourth. The fifth grazed Auguste's forehead.

Avril flung her body on Auguste's. "Stop! Stop it!" she yelled. "Are you crazy?" A flung stick cracked against her knees.

"That's my daughter!" came a voice pitched high with panic. It was Madame Cresson. She hurled her stout body forward and Auguste saw his single chance. He thrust Avril to one side and darted through the passage the woman had momentarily caused.

71

The crowd swerved as if on a turntable. Mesmerized, they watched the boy disappear up the road. Then someone shouted, "After him! He's the devil!"

Released and wild as a wolf pack, they charged after him.

Avril was one of the last to join the mob where Auguste's flight had led them. A weakness in her legs did not permit her to run and her heart thudded against her ribs. So when she arrived Monsieur Hilaire's house was already on fire. When the boy had taken refuge inside, two villagers had started it. Too late to be stopped, the flames had twisted the window frames of the second story, left the long living room a gutted hollow of scarlet and orange; there was one last moment of wholeness before the inner beams crashed.

The girl shoved the people that blocked her way with no concern if they fell or pushed back at her. "Where is Auguste? Where is he?" she cried out over and over. "Auguste! Auguste!"

"The boy's inside," a man answered. And as if his statement commenced a contagion of shame, the crowd began to dissolve, to back off. It turned and started up the road in retreat.

Avril leaped onto the terrace but the solid heat of the flames repelled her. She wished desperately she were in there with her friend, a part of his agony, his death. Alone, she looked upward. There on the roof, his arms outstretched like an eagle about to skim into space, stood Auguste. The distant whiteness of his face seemed to her to be illumined by another light than the fire. Then, like a vision, he vanished.

That night rain fell on the dried fields and gardens. The crops revived and the washed leaves on the trees glistened in the fresh coolness of the wind.

❧ *Eight* ❧

It was three days, Gustave recovering, and the guilt of the villagers decimated into uneasy gossip where the words "witchcraft" and "accident" were much more often used than "murder," before Avril could make herself get out of bed and leave the house. She was civil to her parents and whomever else spoke to her, but even this surface politeness came out of her mouth with difficulty. Her father and mother seemed somehow pleased at this return to her habitual and unidentifiable illness. And no one spoke to her of the fire or Auguste.

The Mayor was seen in the café on Sunday at his usual table with the two women. Madame Fer had hired a new worker and her sole complaint was the amount of money she had to pay him. Madame Cresson responded to inquiries about the health of her daughter with the same stale sighs of former years. Only Avril seemed to remember, and this day she walked out into the sunlight on a pilgrimage.

There was no vitality in her steps as she took to the

road, and the nearer she came to the place where had been her secret source of joy the more reluctant her legs seemed to take her there. But there was one last thing she could do for Auguste. She went directly to the chestnut tree where the medallion was buried. She dug under the turf with both hands and located the shallow hole that now was a grave. Gently she lifted the box from its wrapping of coarse paper and stood erect.

For the first time since the fire she looked straight at the black and gray ruin of Monsieur Hilaire's house. She did not allow herself to ignore any section of it. One half of the façade was still upright, the French doors gone, their glass panes smoked and splintered shards. The chimney at the rear of the ash-filled living room remained, its old stones smeared and cracked. And at the very back of the roofless wreck was the stove, and on it one blistered soup pot.

Then, just as she was about to abandon this grief of a home, a shape like a shadow entered onto the terrace. It began to dance. Slow and slow in a kind of ceremonial pattern whose lines were rigid with antiquity. Then she saw the shadow truly, in three dimensions. It wove itself into a solemn series of interlocking circles that grew smaller and smaller until it arrived at a natural halt. Its arms lifted toward the sky, then the hands joined, palms flat together and the dancer's head lifted and let the sunlight make it visible.

Avril recognized Auguste, she recognized that this was his honoring of Monsieur Hilaire, his farewell to a friend.

She called his name, her voice soft as a dandelion. He

opened his closed eyes and looked at her. His face was as pale as the moon and as faraway.

"Auguste. I believed you were dead."

His head moved in a slow negative.

Strangely, there was no joy in Avril but a suspension of any feeling at all. This was not the same boy who had brought her into life and had taught her what to find there. He seemed to have loaned himself to this last act.

"Auguste," she said again, seeing how his clothes were almost burned off him. "Gustave is better, but how about you? What will you do? Where will you go?"

She knew that to the village he was a true outcast now, not just the mute farm boy, the property of Madame Fer, but someone to be feared and hunted.

For reply he raised one hand in a tiny movement of farewell and reentered the ruins.

Auguste knew she would not follow. She loved him too much to intrude. He stumbled on an ash-covered stone. He fell. He did not try to get up. It would not be a long wait. Perhaps this was the moment to shutter his sight. There was nothing left to look at. But before he accepted the darkness he gazed one last time at what remained of the giant mirror on the wall. The great sliver seemed gradually to reflect a growing light and at the center formed a figure—a tall, spare man whose very stillness was grace. He beckoned to the boy to rise. Auguste obeyed.

Then, as on that far-ago day in another mood, another country, he demonstrated the very first exercise. Auguste took the position and imitated him. He was no longer aware of the terrible tiredness that dragged at him or of the burning of his skin or of the unwillingness of his spirit. From the first, through the whole set of ten, he retraced the discipline of the lessons, and when he was done there was no surprise in him that Monsieur Hilaire had disappeared.

He walked from the house to Avril who had not moved. He seemed somehow taller.

For a moment they looked into each other's eyes. They smiled, together.

Avril held out the velvet box. "Take it," she said. "It's yours."

It passed with tenderness from the girl to the boy. Auguste tucked it into the security of his belt.

Then, placing his hands on her shoulders, he bent down and kissed her.

She watched him go. She watched him turn twice and wave, and though his image diminished and was finally blinked out in a dazzle of sunlight, she knew that wherever he went in the world, whatever happened, he would never be truly gone.

The magic now belonged to him, the magician.